For schoolteachers everywhere
—J.M.

For Kelsey Holinka
—W.W.

Text copyright © 2012 by Jean Marzollo.
"Arts & Crafts" from *I Spy: A Book of Picture Riddles* © 1992 by Walter Wick; "Circus Band" from *I Spy Fun House* © 1993 by Walter Wick; "Chain Reaction" from *I Spy Mystery* © 1993 by Walter Wick; "1, 2, 3...," "A Is for...," "Chalkboard Fun," "Mapping," and "Stegosaurus" from *I Spy School Days* © 1995 by Walter Wick; "The Rainbow Express" from *I Spy Fantasy* © 1994 by Walter Wick; "View from Duck Pond Inn" from *I Spy Treasure Hunt* © 1999 by Walter Wick.

Library of Congress Cataloging-in-Publication Data is available.

ISBN 978-0-545-40281-1

10 9 8 7 6 5 4 3 2   12 13 14 15 16

Printed in the U.S.A. 40 • First printing, July 2012

I SPY
SCHOOL

Riddles by Jean Marzollo
Photographs by Walter Wick

Cartwheel
·B·O·O·K·S· ®

SCHOLASTIC INC.
New York Toronto London Auckland
Sydney Mexico City New Delhi Hong Kong

I spy

a school bus,

 a bright blue van,

a yellow speedboat,

 and a policeman.

I spy

scissors,

a small red rose,

a roll of tape,

and a puppy's black nose

I spy

 a whistle,

a hammer,

 a ship,

a piece of chalk,

 and a paper clip.

I spy

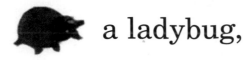 a ladybug,

a silver key,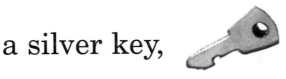

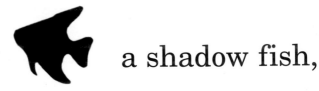 a shadow fish,

an R, R

E and an E.

I spy

a ruler,

an egg that's cracking,

a pencil point,

and a T. rex attacking.

Brian J.

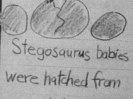

I like the stegasauru because it has spikes on its tail.

Carrie

Stegosaurus babies were hatched from eggs. like reptiles.

CANADA

Utah ★Wyoming
★Colorado
★Oklahoma

Mexico

Stars show where Stegosauruses were found. Toby

A Dinosaur Dig

Fossils show what the bones were like. Paleontologists are the people who like to dig them out of the rocks and study them.
Roberto

I spy

a fountain,

 a statue on a spool,

and a boy running,

perhaps to school.

I spy

 a log,

a cooking-pot handle,

 a yellow triangle,

and a birthday candle.

I spy

a cave,

 a ball cap to wear,

a school's banner,

 and a polar bear.

I spy

 a race car,

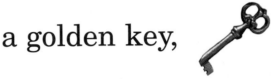 a golden key,

 seven books,

and a big green 3.

I spy

a paintbrush,

a pencil that's blue,

a red pushpin,

and a gold star for you.

I spy 2 matching words.

school bus

ruler

boy running,

perhaps to school

I spy 2 matching words.

pencil that's blue

bright blue van

polar bear

I spy 3 words that start with the letter S.

seven books

 silver key

school's banner

I spy 2 words that start with the letters SP.

 yellow speedboat

egg that's cracking

 statue on a spool

I spy 3 words that end with the letter G.

ladybug

log

T. rex attacking

I spy 2 words that end with the letters SH.

shadow fish

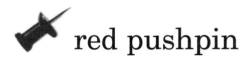 red pushpin

paintbrush

I spy a word and a letter that rhyme.

R R

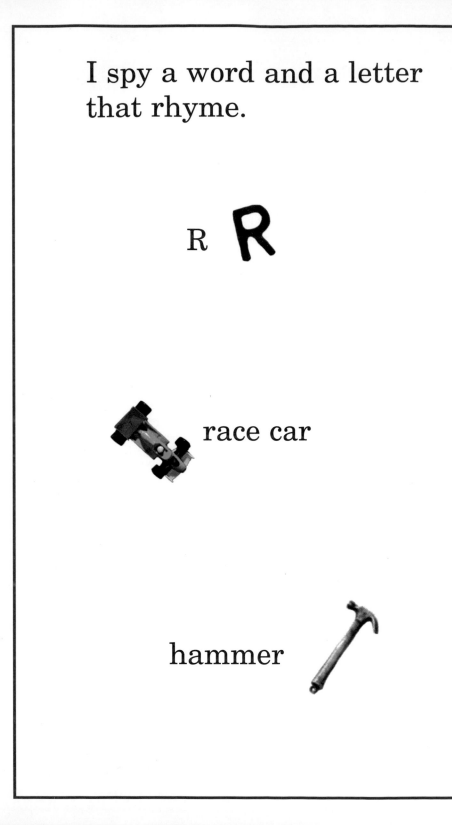 race car

hammer

I spy 2 words that rhyme.

 small red rose

ball cap to wear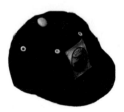

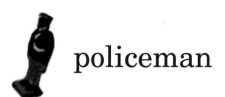 policeman